The Aftermath

Book 1

My New Normal

Sara Michelle

D0964855

SADDLEBACK
EDUCATIONAL PUBLISHING

My New Normal

The Aftermath * Book 1
The Inside * Book 2
The Others * Book 3

SADDLEBACK℠
EDUCATIONAL PUBLISHING
www.sdlback.com

ISBN-13: 978-1-61651-770-0
ISBN-10: 1-61651-770-0
eBook: 978-1-61247-350-5

Printed in Guangzhou, China
0911/CA21101549

16 15 14 13 12   1 2 3 4 5

Day 7

I almost wish I hadn't made it. At least then I'd be dead. I don't really know what happens after we die. But I know it would sure beat this situation I've found myself in. Still, I don't think I'll ever fully grasp how lucky we are to be alive—if you can call it luck. I sometimes find myself thinking that it would've been so much easier to have passed away. I think being dead would be easier than this new life—my new normal.

It was freezing. It felt as if the sun had lost every joule of heat. Sure it was shining bright—a little too bright given the tragedy. But the air was angry, frigid. This was the kind of cold that couldn't be eliminated with sweatpants and fuzzy slippers. This was the kind of cold you got when you had the flu. Not even the hottest bath could make you feel warm enough. The wind penetrated your brain, and every breath you took turned your blood to ice. Our throats were raw.

Finding a decent heat source was nearly impossible. All the power was out here along with the rest of the city. And the state. And the country. At this point I wouldn't have been surprised if the entire planet had been damaged by this catastrophe.

There were no civil humans around. All the people left were fighting for their lives. We were all looking for the same things. Food, water, shelter, and more importantly, an answer to this mess.

Ryan and I kept to ourselves. Thank God I've got him. Pure fate kept us together, that's for sure. From what we've calculated, it's been seven days since *The End*. We don't really have a more suitable name for it right now.

There was absolutely no warning. Quite frankly, I don't think anyone expected anything out of the ordinary to happen. It was three days after Christmas. The only thing unusual was the clear sky. Typically, we're pelted with snow at this time of year. But it was cold and sunny. Perfect holiday weather.

We'd just finished celebrating Christmas. Our two-year anniversary was a short two days away. Then our entire lives were shaken—literally. This earthquake was no ordinary earthquake. I'd grown up in California, and I'd experienced what I thought was the worst. But this was no California quake. It was as if the Lord himself had shaken the earth with every bit of power he held. Every bone in your body rattled and collided. Pain soared through your joints and nerves. Frantic screams could be heard; small explosions, then larger ones.

I do remember seeing panic sweep across Ryan's face. Then darkness. But I'll never fully remember or know how terrifying that day really was. I was completely unconscious for two days after it happened.

I awoke to Ryan's gentle embrace. That must have been on day three. He was stroking my hair. I remember it being so bitterly cold. After my eyes adjusted, I was hit with a painful dose of reality. This was no dream. No ordinary nightmare either. This was real. This was hell on earth.

The city looked like a creepy ghost town from a cheesy cable movie. Every building in eyesight was destroyed and covered in a blanket of ash and gray snow. Every once in a while, a crazed survivor could be seen, running, calling out, looking for help. Their cries were left unanswered.

We were alone and scared. Nobody

expected the theories and stories to actually come true. I think that people had put the thought of the apocalypse out of their minds. After 2012 passed with no strange activity, the whole idea seemed like rubbish. Seemed like a lifetime away. We were proven terribly wrong. Nostradamus got it right after all. The earth had played a sickening joke, caving into itself, destroying everything it could. Now here we were with no idea of where to go or what was yet to come.

It continued to get colder. I prayed that the weather stayed clear. A blizzard would kill off every last survivor. We were able to find some torn blankets and dirty coats in the midst of all the rubble. They were filthy and smelled of death and raw sewage. But hygiene would have to come after warmth. Cold meant death.

I hadn't bathed since it happened. I'm sure I looked like a monster. My hair felt dry and caked with mud and other unknown garbage. I was bruised and cut from the impact of the quake. My mouth was dry. I could taste vomit. But I didn't complain. I needed to be thankful. Not only for the fact that I was alive, but because I was alive with Ryan. He doesn't fail to rock me to sleep each miserable night, and I know he's not going to leave me. Yes, I can say I'm grateful.

We walked past a young boy today, probably around seven years old. I'll never know how he made it. His blue eyes stood out like jewels against his bruised body. The look of terror and bewilderment on his face caused my heart to ache. I looked at Ryan with pleading eyes. He shook his head.

"Cecilia," he said taking my hand, "he won't make it. At this point, it'd only frustrate him and slow us down. We don't know what happens next, and we can't take risks. It's every man for himself."

He was right. We couldn't have any extra baggage on our hands. But I looked at the boy with sympathy. I wondered how he felt. Was he confused? Well I guess that was obvious. Where was his mom? How was his life before … this? I almost began to argue with Ryan's decision, but reality set in.

Emotionally I was drained. My body ached from being shaken to its core. My stomach longed for food. My throat was dry and thirsted for water. The snow was too dirty to touch. We had to walk. We had to figure out the severity of the situation. We needed food. We needed water. We needed shelter. So far, we'd only come across moldy food and dirty water. I'd tried drinking some, but it only made me sick. Other than that, we'd only found more dirt, mangled bodies, and the rubble of what used to be. It seemed as if someone had come and stolen all the necessary items to live.

Day 8

"Cecilia, honey, wake up." Ryan shook me gently and I groaned. Everything ached. My eyelids felt like weights. I shivered. Ryan pulled me closer. His heart thumped against my cheek, assuring me that life still ran through his veins. Without him I'd be gone. I wouldn't try to live. But I wouldn't give up until he did. I couldn't. He'd already done so much for me, and I would never leave him to face this alone.

We lay there for a while, just listening to each other breathing. After a couple minutes, just as I began dozing off again, his voice woke me up.

"I have an idea," he stated. I looked up at him. His beach-blond hair brushed against his rosy cheeks. His blue eyes sparkled with determination.

"Well what is it?" I asked. My stomach growled. He winced and looked at me with a certain sort of helplessness.

"It just seems impossible that everything here is gone. I mean … obviously … we aren't going to find anything in perfect shape. But I just don't think we'd still be alive if we had no chance. It just doesn't seem right. There *has* to be somewhere or something that can provide us with the necessities," Ryan said.

"But everything is totally demolished!" I couldn't believe what I was hearing.

Ryan kept talking. "Snow shelters are made to withhold the strongest blizzards. The poles that secure them extend at least 30 feet under the ground or maybe more. They keep blankets, canned goods, and who knows what else there. If we're lucky, maybe the backup power will be running. I know they use solar energy for the generator and water pump. I mean, I'm sure the shelter isn't in perfect condition. But most of it is underground. Look at the state we're in, we'll take whatever we can get. It's worth a shot."

I thought a moment. The Denver Snow Shelter was a good twenty-minute drive. With the condition the city was in, walking would take days. How were we going to walk through the layers of snow … the torn-up sidewalks … the cracked and pitted streets? I wondered if I was physically able to make it. I knew my time was limited. I could feel my body begin to shut down. Tears filled my eyes. Ryan pulled me into a tight grasp. We sat there, intertwined. It was silent around us. Too silent.

"Cecilia," he whispered. I turned and looked up at him. He took a deep breath, "I'm not going to give up until I know you're okay. To make sure that you're well and healthy, I'll carry you as many miles as I have to. I'd promise that everything is going to work out, but … I just … I don't know."

It was his turn to look away. Ryan had always been the strong one. After his father left, he was always the man of the house. He didn't let anything get to him. I knew he was shattered. I turned his chin toward me. Silent tears rolled down his cheeks. I wiped them away and tried to smile.

"We're going to do this. We're going to find what we need. Who knows? Maybe the survivors will crown us king and queen of the world," I smirked.

He rolled his eyes. My lame sense of humor always made him smile. I couldn't give him up. We needed each other now more than ever.

Day 9

We're exhausted. If I could, I'd fall to the ground right now and take a nap. But I really don't know if I'd wake up. I'm sick to my stomach. But there's no food in it to throw up. I feel as if my body is eating itself up as a last resort. We've made progress. And by that I mean the scenery has changed. I think we're near where the chapel used to be. If we'd been in a car, and the world hadn't fallen apart on top of us, we'd be about ten minutes away.

I'd thought about asking Ryan why we couldn't try to find a car to use. But then once again, reality hit me. If we did find a working car, what were the chances we'd find the keys? And nearly all the gas stations had blown up during the earthquake. But we could drive as far as we could on the gas in the car, right? Wrong. The streets were really torn up. We'd need an urban assault vehicle to clear the rubble. Nobody was plowing the streets either, so the route was basically impassable. But honestly, if walking through the night meant food and rest tomorrow, I'd do it. Walking wasn't so bad. It actually kept you somewhat warm.

We saw more people today. They were in worse shape than we were though. One lady was lying down screaming for help. Blood covered her. Ryan said not to go near her. We didn't know what diseases were around. We couldn't risk getting more exposed to them than we already were. And besides, there was nothing we could do to help. She would surely freeze by morning.

It was sad but true. We saw a lot of frozen corpses. And I wondered how the survivors would carry on without modern medicine … I knew there were healing herbs and stuff, but who was left who would know?

How does society begin again from absolutely nothing? I mean, it seemed like we were back in the middle ages. These were all questions I couldn't wait to get answers to. Then again, I wondered whether or not we'd make it far enough to find them.

We had to stop to rest tonight. Ryan became violently ill about halfway through our journey to the snow shelter. I really thought I was going to lose him. He began turning paler. Then his breathing became shallow. I told him to sit down, and he didn't argue. I really thought that he was just tired. I thought that it'd blow over after resting for a little while. But it got worse. His eyes began to glaze over. He began having a coughing fit. I have never felt so helpless in my life. I held his hand and tried to talk him through it. But he just coughed and coughed. Finally, the coughing started to ease up. His eyes were red, and he'd popped a blood vessel in his right eye from coughing so much. He looked horrible.

"Do you think you're actually sick with the flu or something?" I asked cautiously. If he had caught something, we were doomed.

He took a deep breath and looked up at me with weary eyes. "I don't think so. But I don't really know, Cecilia. I'm just so tired, and I am so frustrated. I think it's just stress and strain. But I don't know. So I don't think you should get too close to me."

I shook my head. I wasn't leaving his side. Not even for a second. Because if he died, I'd die. And I wasn't trying to be cheesy or dramatic—typical girl stuff.

It was just the truth. I'd have no idea what to do or where to go. Everyone I knew was dead except Ryan. My heart would be broken to pieces if anything happened to him. I grabbed his hand.

"Ryan, I'm staying here right next to you. For better or for worse."

He smiled. "I'm going to marry you the second we figure out this mess. It's the first thing on my list when we start our new lives together."

I squeezed his hand. Even in the midst of all this destruction and disaster, he never failed to make my heart race. I really did love him.

"What can I do to make you better?" I asked him.

He coughed again. I winced. He looked around. We were in the middle of what was once a pretty wealthy neighborhood. The houses now were nearly or completely destroyed. It seemed as if they'd been made out of clay and someone had stepped directly on them. He was lying on what looked like it used to be a front porch. The house beyond was in pieces. Its neighbor was in better shape than any other house on the block, or any other house we'd seen on our journey. It was just barely standing. It leaned to the right, and some shutters were hanging by single screws. But it looked somewhat promising.

"I'm going to check that house out," I told him pointing next door. He tried to sit up and look at it. I gently pushed him down. "Stay here."

I stood up and dusted some of the grime off of my jeans. I shivered. It seemed to be getting even colder. Ryan looked up at me with weary eyes. He smiled.

"What?" I asked him. He shook his head.

"You just never fail to amaze me," he said. "You are so beautiful."

I rolled my eyes, astounded at his comment. I didn't even want to look in a mirror. I'm sure I looked like a wreck. Who wouldn't? I patted his leg and started walking to the neighboring house.

I approached the house with caution. I had no idea what I was getting myself into. What if the family that had lived in this house before was still here, buried underneath all the rubble? Or what if the people who had lived here before were sick with some sort of contagious disease? I couldn't prepare myself enough. I took a deep breath. This was for Ryan. He needed to get well. It was worth every risk in the book to find him somewhere to sleep and recover. Because if I lost him, I lost everything.

I walked over the piles of dirt and rocks and snow and approached where the front door would've stood. It was lying a couple feet inside the house— totally cracked in half. The interior was completely trashed. Surprisingly the couch was still intact but flipped over onto its side. But the smell ... I held back a wave of nausea. The house reeked of rotten food. And a certain other smell. Death? Possibly. But I couldn't worry about that. We'd passed enough corpses already that I was almost getting used to the idea of dead bodies. How sick was that?

I stepped over a couple ripped pillows and pieces of wood. I found two blankets in the corner of the room. They were covered in dirt and dust but still in one piece. Hope welled inside of me. We could flip the couch and use the blankets and pillows. He'd be able to sleep and get better. I was starting to feel okay about the situation.

I wondered what else I'd be lucky enough to find. I wandered into what would've been the kitchen. The smell of moldy and rotten food grew.

I gagged. I didn't have much hope for food, but I decided to check the pantry just in case. Broken glass was everywhere. Exploded canned goods littered their contents over the floor. It smelled of beans and pickles. I ignored the squishing beneath my feet and browsed through the bags of snack food on the floor. I nearly shrieked in excitement as I pulled up a bag of Fritos. Fritos!

It was open and some dirt had seeped in, but there were still enough chips to share with Ryan. It wasn't much, but it was something. My stomach growled. I would have to wait. Ryan needed to get better first. I looked around some more. But I didn't find anything that would be considered edible.

I tried to keep my hopes up. This was definitely more than I bargained for. I walked back out of the kitchen and took a deep breath. I couldn't wait to tell Ryan about my discoveries. I walked back through the living area and outside. Amazingly, it seemed to have gotten even colder than when I entered the house. I shivered. Ryan was where I'd left him, lying on the old porch. He sat up when he heard me coming.

"Ryan, we can sleep in that house tonight. There's a roof and a couch. We just need to flip it over! And there are a couple blankets too!"

He looked at me and smiled. "Thank goodness," he nearly whispered.

I took his hand and helped him

stand up. He shut his eyes and wobbled. I put my arm around him and led him into the house next door. He shut his eyes tight when the smell hit him.

"I think I'm going to be sick," he muttered. He bent down and was suddenly violently ill.

After what seemed like minutes, he stood back up. His eyes were dilated, and he was even paler than he was before. My heart dropped to my feet. I was filled with dread. It didn't look like things were going to get much better. I stared at him. I was terrified.

"I'll be fine," he croaked.

I shook my head. He wasn't fine.

I walked over and picked up the two blankets the earthquake left uncovered. I shook them out and put them aside.

I knew I wasn't going to be able to lift that couch by myself. Ryan coughed and walked over to the couch with me. He winced as he tried to lift it.

"Let me go on the other side, Ryan. I'll help you. We'll turn it on the count of three."

He nodded.

I walked over and grabbed the other edge of the couch. I placed my hands underneath it and braced myself.

"One ... two ... three!" I said.

On three we both grunted and flipped the couch over. It was filthy. It was covered in dirt and little shards of glass. I was going to have to clean it before he could get settled. I began sweeping off the glass. But Ryan put his hand up and shook his head.

"Babe, enough. This is going to be just fine. I just need to lie down."

I stopped and moved out of the way. He grabbed one of the blankets and laid it down on top of the couch. Then he slowly settled himself.

"This is the most comfortable I've been all week," he sighed.

All week? Had it really been a week since that devastating day? Time was moving fast. Which meant our time was running out. We needed drinkable water and some protein. I had a feeling the Fritos weren't going to help much.

I watched as Ryan almost immediately fell into a deep sleep. I watched him sleep. I watched his chest move up and down. It was my reassurance that he was still alive. That we were still here. That this wasn't a dream. I was afraid to turn my head, because what if … what if he just happened to stop breathing? My heart broke at the thought of losing him—at the thought of being completely alone in this new world that had been cast upon us. I wasn't even capable of thinking about it without crying. I had no idea what I would do.

I tried to shove all the negative thoughts to the back of my head and figure out whether or not I should try and sleep for a while. If so, should I sleep next to Ryan or on the floor? That wasn't a hard one. There was no way I was going to sleep on the floor. I stood up and slowly walked over to my peacefully sleeping boyfriend.

The color had begun to return to his cheeks, and his breathing didn't sound so labored. I began to relax. Sleep was all we needed. We needed to clear our thoughts and rest our aching bodies.

I was suddenly overcome with complete exhaustion. I crawled next to Ryan under the blanket. I rested my cheek against his chest and felt immediately at ease. I quickly found myself falling into a deep, peaceful sleep.

I was in my room. In my house. Before hell had taken over. Ryan and I were sitting on my bed working on our junior AP Chemistry homework. Chemistry was not my thing, but Ryan was in the class. He loved coming over to help me with homework. The smell of lasagna and garlic bread rose from the kitchen where our moms happily cooked and gossiped. They were the best of friends and enjoyed every excuse to be together. It always amazed us how both our dads had left. It gave us all an immediate connection with each other. Ryan's mom and my mom had so much in common. They spent a lot of the time dissing their exes and discussing how Ryan was going to be the right kind of gentleman. It was somewhat sad but somewhat humorous, and it's what brought us all that much closer.

Suddenly we were all piled on Ryan's couch watching *Grey's Anatomy*. The moms were looking at Christmas catalogs. Ryan and I were eating popcorn, watching the show, and discussing our plans for the Christmas holidays. The smell of chocolate chip cookies filled my nose.

I slowly opened my eyes. There were no baking cookies. Things weren't going to ever be the same again. Our moms were probably dead. Our friends were probably dead. Ryan would never greet me in the hallways of our high school. He wouldn't leave me notes in my locker. And he wouldn't pick me up after cheer practice. High school was over. Reality was a bitter pill. I drifted back into a confused and haunted sleep.

Day 10

I woke up to the sound of birds. For some reason, this really threw me off. The chirps and melodies reminded me of my old normal life. I guess I didn't realize that maybe some animals had survived the earthquake too. I opened my eyes and felt better than I had in days. I wondered how long we'd slept.

I turned over. Ryan was gone. Fear welled up inside of me. I quickly sat up and looked around. We were still in the house, or at least I was. Ryan was nowhere to be seen or heard. I wondered if he left me. I knew it was silly, but it was awfully strange of him to leave me here alone. I stretched and yawned. My mouth felt disgusting. I really wanted a toothbrush.

"Morning sunshine," Ryan greeted me. He looked great. Healthy, almost. The color had returned to his face, and he even looked cleaner.

"Where were you? What time is it?" I asked. I was a little freaked out. But I also wanted to sleep more.

He smiled. I felt way better.

"I'm pretty sure it's almost three. I don't have a watch, but I just have that afternoon feeling," he said. "I don't know if we slept through an entire day or not. I just woke up a couple hours ago and decided to do some more exploring and scavenging. It paid off. Look what I found."

He pulled from behind his back a pack of saltines and three bottles of water. This was a huge find! My stomach growled. He laughed and sat next to me on the couch. He handed me a bottle of water, which I gulped down with intense speed. I was so sick of trying to melt dirty snow to drink. The water felt so good on my throat and in my stomach. I felt refreshed. He opened the saltines and began eating. I joined him. We sat there in silence, eating and drinking. My body thanked me. I felt the blood begin to pump through my muscles again, and my stomach was finally somewhat satisfied. Sure, it wasn't the sirloin steak dinner I was craving, but it was something. And something was good.

After we were done munching on our feast, I lay back on the couch. Did I say how refreshed I felt? I didn't even mind that I hadn't showered or changed my clothes. My insides were clean. I was clear-minded and ready to decide what to do next.

Ryan looked at me and took a deep breath. I smiled and decided to see what our plan was.

"So what's the plan, baby? What adventures do we go on next?" I asked.

It was his turn to smile. He started, "I think we should still try and head for the snow shelter. It's going to be our best bet for right now."

I agreed. Yet I was still sort of un-
nerved at the thought of leaving this
house. I felt safe here. It was almost
home. For a while I'd forgotten about
the horrors outside that doorframe.
And that was worth everything to me.
But I knew we had to move on. I just
had a hard time accepting it.

"Are we going to start walking today?" I asked him, sort of hoping he'd
say no.

He turned and looked outside. The
sun was shining bright, but you could
tell it was pretty late in the afternoon.
I hated walking at night, and Ryan
knew that.

"I don't think it'd hurt to stay
one more night here. I think another
night's rest would help us be that much

more prepared for the journey tomorrow. Don't you agree?" He looked at me smiling. I nodded my head. I couldn't agree more.

Day 11

I woke up feeling great. My muscles were fully relaxed, and my growling stomach wasn't my alarm clock. I turned over and looked at Ryan, who was still sleeping soundly, a small grin on his face. He was so cute. I couldn't believe how lucky I was to have him. I laid my head back down and stared at the ceiling.

I thought about our future. Not just within the next couple days, or weeks, or even months. I thought about how humanity was going to cope with this worldwide disaster. I wondered how we'd start up again. How was technology going to be revived? I wondered how we were going to get the brains to make medicine again, to reestablish some sort of government. It was beyond the scope of two teenagers from the suburbs. I thought AP Chemistry was hard!

I thought about the Mayans. They'd been completely wiped out. Greed. Corruption. Drought. Civilization as they knew it—gone. Is this how other civilizations disappeared? I had so many unanswered questions. But only in time would we be able to figure it out.

Ryan began stirring. I shut my eyes quickly, not wanting him to know that

I was already awake. I still wasn't too keen on the idea of leaving, although I knew it had to be done. Ryan placed his hand on my arm and shook me gently. I opened my eyes and saw him looking at me … smiling.

"You're so cute when you pretend to be asleep."

I rolled my eyes and laughed. He knew me too well.

"We should get going, Cecilia. I know you don't want to leave, but we're going to need way more resources than what we've got here."

"Yeah, yeah. I know," I said.

I rolled off the couch and stood up to stretch. Although I was feeling better than I had in days, I still felt insanely dirty.

"Ryan is there *any* chance of running water here?"

He shook his head. "Cecilia, no. Especially not here. Really, I know you feel nasty. So do I. So let's get walking. The snow shelter could be the answer to our prayers."

I groaned. I longed for a long, hot shower. I was so tired of all of this.

I felt Ryan's arms wrap around my waist. I didn't know how he could touch me. I felt filthy. And I know I looked as bad as I felt.

"You're beautiful," he whispered in my ear. I shook my head. Lies. He kissed my cheek. "You really are. Always have been, always will be. No matter what. Let's go."

I turned and looked him in the eye.

He had the prettiest blue eyes. He kissed me on the lips. I never got tired of that. We looked at each other and smiled.

"Let's go!" I said enthusiastically. I was in a much better mood now. I just wanted to get there.

He took my hand and we walked out of the doorway. Hello reality.

Things hadn't improved outside. It was still as cold as ever, and nobody had emerged from the destroyed neighborhood. I wondered if they had all fled somewhere, or if they really were all … dead. The thought gave me the chills. Could a whole modern-day city really be wiped off the face of the earth? It was horrifying just to consider it.

"How long do you think we're going

to have to walk from here?" I asked. I really hoped it wasn't long. I hated it out here. There was too much death. It was just a reminder of how scary this situation really was.

Ryan looked out toward the direction we were headed. The drive to the snow shelter was usually not very long from here. But with all the destruction ... the way things were torn up ... walking would probably take us most of the day.

"I think that if we don't run into any issues, we should get there sometime tonight. But I honestly have no idea what we might encounter. Lucky for us, it looks like the weather is holding."

I really hoped we wouldn't *encounter*

anything. I just wanted to be there already.

We walked and walked for what seemed like hours. And it was. But we still hadn't come across anything too bad. We saw a couple of older women crying near a completely trashed house. But that was it. The city was deserted.

The really eerie thing was the fact that it was nearly dead silent. We were used to the usual bustling city sounds, but the only sounds that we could hear were occasional birds. It was cold and quiet. Usually the daylight would add more reassurance, but it only made things more unsettling. It was proof that silence was indeed one of the loudest sounds. I held onto Ryan's arm as we walked through the abandoned city that had once been our home.

The journey seemed to drag on and on. I was starting to feel weak again, and I was beginning to really wish we'd just stayed at the other house. What if the snow shelter was in the same state as everything else we'd seen? What would we do then? It all began to just seem completely pointless to me. I tried to keep my thoughts to myself because I didn't want to drag Ryan down. He was trying to stay positive, and I didn't want to be a Debbie Downer anymore than I already had been.

After a while I decided to go ahead and ask how much progress we'd made. "How much longer you think it'll be?"

Ryan looked around us and thought for a minute. "At the rate we're going, and assuming we don't have any encounters," he smiled, "I'm guessing an hour or two. Are you doing okay?"

I wanted to cry like a baby and sit down. But I needed to grow up. If this was how life was going to be for a while, I needed to toughen up a lot.

"Doing great! Actually, I was hoping it'd take longer."

Ryan rolled his eyes and laughed. I held his hand and kept walking. I took a deep breath. I could do this.

I kind of wished I had an iPod or at least a radio. Or even Ryan's guitar. He'd actually gotten pretty good at playing before the earthquake. It made me sad to think he may never play the guitar again.

The scenery around us began to change a little bit. There weren't as many houses. When we did come across one, it was totally demolished. I wondered how the families were that had lived in these homes. Were they even alive?

Just when I began to drift off into another train of thought, I heard voices speaking. I thought I was going insane, so I looked up at Ryan to see if he'd heard them too. He had. We paused our walking and looked around. The voices seemed to be coming from behind. We turned in the direction and saw two older women sitting on a pile of rubble. One of the women was crying hysterically. The other seemed to be trying to calm her down. They hadn't noticed us.

"What are we going to do?" I whispered.

"I think we should just keep walking. We shouldn't get ourselves involved with anyone until we figure out a definite plan for the next week or so. Just walk quietly."

I complied, and we started moving again.

"Hey, you!" one of the women called out. I peeked over at Ryan who had his lips pursed tightly. He tightened his grip on my hand and slowly turned around.

"Yes, ma'am?" he called back.

"Come here! Please!" she called desperately.

"Let's just keep walking, Ryan," I whispered. I didn't want to deal with anyone right now. Although I knew how selfish that sounded, I looked at him with pleading eyes.

"I'm just going to see what she wants," he whispered. "Do you want to come or stay here?"

I bit my lip. I didn't want to go but wasn't going to stand there by myself looking like an idiot.

We held hands and walked toward the two women. The one who was standing had on destroyed jeans that I knew she didn't buy that way. She had wild red hair that stood straight up on her head. She looked around my mom's age with bags under her bright green eyes.

"Yes, ma'am?" Ryan asked politely.

"What has happened here?" she cried.

I realized with surprise that she had an accent that sounded European.

"I can't tell you for sure, ma'am. I really don't know," he said.

The lady who was crying stopped. She looked up at us curiously. She was younger than the redhead but looked only a little bit older than Ryan and me. She had long brunette hair that hung past her waist. Her eyes were a dark brown and her skin was porcelain white. She was gorgeous even in the state she was in.

"Well, how can we get home?" the older lady moaned. "We are visiting from Italy, and we need to go home now."

I almost rolled my eyes. Could she not understand that there was absolutely no way she was getting back home? Ever. Then I began to wonder again if the whole world had been devastated. Probably. Yes, it had to have been demolished. If not, the area would be crawling with rescue teams.

"I'm afraid you aren't going to be able to get home for a long time. Based on how things look around here," Ryan pointed to the ruins of downtown in the distance. "I'm sure that the airport and airlines have been destroyed. Look at the rest of the city. There's nothing there. You're just going to have to wait for further help because there's nothing we can do."

The younger girl began crying again. "Obnoxious," I mumbled. "Get a grip."

I was about to start getting really pissed. I knew these people were foreign tourists or whatever. But if we couldn't keep the little boy who needed help, why were we dealing with this? These ladies could fend for themselves.

The older lady stared at Ryan and then at me.

"Well, what are you two going to do then? Just walk around aimlessly?" she asked.

I glared at her. She really didn't want to make me any more mad than I already was. I knew I was being heartless, but I couldn't help it.

I felt Ryan take a deep breath, and I knew that he was trying not to lose it too. I hoped he was regretting coming over here.

"We're just trying to deal with everything. I don't know what we're going to do, but I think you two should just wait for help," he said.

The younger girl stopped crying again and looked at Ryan. She looked at the older lady and began talking in a completely different language. The older one snapped something back. Then they both looked at us.

"If you find help, please tell them to come retrieve us. Okay?" the older one barked at Ryan.

I wanted to laugh out loud. This was ridiculous. There were no more princesses in this new world.

"I will do that, ma'am. Have a nice day," Ryan said.

Ryan grabbed my hand and we began walking away. As soon as we left, we could hear the bickering start up again between the two of them.

I began laughing. I laughed like I hadn't laughed since before the earthquake. At first Ryan stopped and looked at me as if I had gone nuts, but pretty soon he cracked a smile and began laughing too. We both laughed until we couldn't breathe. It felt so good to be laughing again.

After we caught our breath, we looked at each other and smiled. Of all the crazy people we could've run into, we ran into two crazy Italians looking for a jet home. I wanted this moment to last forever. But we had to push on.

We walked and walked. Occasionally one of us would say something mimicking the ladies' accents, and we would lose it all over again. In my old normal, I was never this mean. But in this new world it felt good to laugh, and it made the journey much more bearable.

The sun was beginning to set, and I began to worry if we would have to walk through the night. Right when I was going to ask Ryan what he thought, we approached the gate to the snow shelter. Happiness welled inside of me.

"Finally!" I cried, jumping up and down.

The snow shelter was located past a gate and on top of a small hill. From what we could see, the outside of the shelter was beaten up. But we were hoping that the inside was going to be okay. We didn't have a plan B.

"I told you it was a good idea!" Ryan said. He was almost as excited as I was. We picked up our pace. It was a tough trek up the snowy road, but ten minutes later we stood in front of the shelter.

The sign was completely destroyed. The doors had been ripped off their hinges. Part of the roof had collapsed. But the walls were still standing. I tried really hard not to get my hopes up. What if people had already thought of this idea? What if all of the supplies were gone? Or what if there weren't

any supplies to begin with? What if
everything was trashed? My mind raced.
I almost didn't even want to walk in.
I couldn't stand the thought of being
disappointed. This was our last shot at
survival.

"Well, let's check it out," Ryan said
as he walked toward the entryway. I
lingered behind and thought about just
staying outside.

"Are you coming, Cecilia?" he
asked.

I sighed and walked up to the front
entry and stood next to Ryan. I peeked
in. Trash was scattered around. Glass
lay smashed on the floor. Huge chunks
of ceiling blocked parts of the hallway.

"From what I've heard about the
snow shelter, there's a staircase that

leads to the basement, which is where the kitchen and the cots are. I think that would be the best bet right now, so let's try to find it."

I couldn't really disagree, so I followed him. We walked past a couple of rooms that looked like they were used as offices. The rooms were a total loss. I really hoped the basement was in better shape. We walked through a couple long corridors and climbed over rubble. Finally we ended up in front of two huge metal doors.

"I'm pretty sure this is the staircase. Do you want to come and look down there with me or stay up here?" he asked.

"I'll follow you," I said. There was no way I was going to be left alone in this creepy place.

He pulled on the doors. Slowly, slowly they opened. The lights in the stairwell flickered. We could hear the hum of a backup generator. It looked like a scene from a scary movie. I cautiously followed him down the stairs. We walked down what seemed like two flights and ended up in front of another door. These doors weren't as heavy and opened easily. The lights in the room were dim. I squinted, trying to adjust to the new lighting.

The room we now stood in was completely furnished. Two red leather couches were in the middle and a small coffee table stood between them. A plasma screen TV was mounted on the wall. Except for a large crack on the screen, it was in perfect shape. There was a wall clock that seemed to work. It looked like the ones that were all over school. Happiness welled up inside of me. Something normal at last! This looked like it was going to work out perfectly.

I looked over at Ryan, who was taking it all in with a dopey smile on his face.

"You were right, babe!" I cried and ran into his arms for a hug. He picked me up and twirled me around. I laughed. I was overjoyed.

"Let's find the showers and see if they work!" he suggested.

I happily agreed. A shower sounded perfect right now. We walked past the living area and into a long hallway.

There were about six doors on each side, which all looked like the doors that got us in here. The shelter seemed completely deserted.

I opened the door closest to me. Inside was a small, twin-sized bed. Completely intact. Oh joy! I screamed and jumped onto the bed like a kid. It was soft and smelled brand new. I couldn't believe our luck. It almost seemed too good to be true. How could this stuff survive the quake? It didn't seem like anything would be able to.

Ryan stood at the doorway with that same dopey smile on his face. I could tell he was just as excited as I was. He was soaking it up.

I scanned the room. There were a couple blankets on the foot of the bed. There was another single door in the room. It was closed. So I walked up and opened it. Inside was a toilet, sink, and a shower. It was a small room, just enough for everything to fit. But it was clean, and there was a shower. A shower! I tried to not get too excited because we still didn't know if the water pipes had survived the earthquake. Ryan peeked in the bathroom. He was still smiling.

"Try the water," he encouraged. "I think they have a water source for the basement with separate pipes. The really cold temperatures of a blizzard would freeze them if they were outside or upstairs."

That was true. I cautiously leaned over and turned the water dial toward hot. It turned on. I shrieked! I was going to be clean. I was going to take a shower ASAP. The water turned from cold, to lukewarm, to hot. It worked perfectly. I turned and gave Ryan another hug. This *was* too good to be true.

"Do you want to shower now? Or check out the rest and come back?" he asked.

I didn't care at all. As long as I got to shower, I didn't care.

"Let's see the food, and then we can come back!" I said as I turned off the water.

We walked out of the room and checked out the others. They were all similar but with a different number of beds in each. One room even had bunk beds. Then we backtracked. Next to the living room was another big room. The kitchen. There were three wall ovens and two refrigerators next to them. A closet was on the other side of the kitchen. Probably the pantry.

I ran over to the fridge and opened it. "There's not much here. There's no produce." My shoulders sagged. I was so disappointed. What if we didn't get food?

"I'll look in this closet, there's got to be something!" Ryan said. He walked over to the closet and opened it. Inside was a pantry about twenty feet deep. Filled with food! Chips, cookies, snacks, canned goods, Tetra Paks of milk, it was all there.

I don't think I've ever felt so relieved. We were going to be okay. At least for the time being. I felt Ryan wrap his arms around my waist. He kissed me on the cheek.

"I think everything is going to be just fine. At least for now. Don't you?" he asked.

I nodded. I didn't even notice the tears rolling down my face until Ryan wiped one off my cheek.

I turned and looked at him. He smiled.

"I really think this is going to be an adventure. I think that instead of calling all of this *The End*, we should call it *The Beginning*."

It was my turn to smile. Just as I turned to kiss him gently on the lips, we heard something upstairs. Something was coming our way. It was indeed the beginning, but the beginning of what?

About the Author

Sara Michelle

As a high school student, I never thought that I could pursue my creative interests. But with the support of my family, I auditioned to attend an arts magnet program in south-central Texas. I'm so excited to be going to a school that lets me explore my right brain and harnesses my imagination.

Speaking of interests ... those would involve: singing, songwriting, dancing, reading, going out with friends, spending money, and—writing. I love this time in my life and plan to live it up while doing what I used to believe was impossible, writing and publishing books. One day I'd love to get my PhD in psychology—and in a parallel universe, I'd love to be an actor. My favorite food is ice cream; I could honestly live off of it 24/7. My friends mean the world to me, and I'd be absolutely nowhere without my large, crazy family. I can't wait to see what life has to offer, and I plan on enjoying every minute of it!

My New Normal

The following is an excerpt

from *Book 2...*

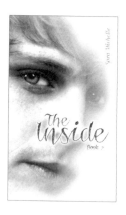

Day 13

8:00 a.m.

I felt my brain slip out of its dream state. It was so comforting to finally wake up in an actual bed. I lay still, appreciating the moment before finally opening my eyes. They slowly opened, and I took in the scenery around me. The room was plain, but it was sturdy, safe, and I was finally able to claim something as my own.

Cecilia and I'd begun to consider the snow shelter as our temporary home. It was the first clean and suitable shelter we had since the earthquake almost two weeks ago. I shuddered at the pang of painful memories. I just didn't want to go there. Not yet. I don't think I could ever thank God enough for keeping me and the love of my life alive and, for the most part, healthy. It definitely wasn't the easiest weeks of my life, but we got through it together and with very little *physical* damage.

I'll never be able to get rid of the horrible memories of that day. The screaming. The boom. The flash of light. The gore. The pain. The complete blood-pumping horror. It was almost too much to bear. No matter how long I live, that day will never stop haunting me.

After traveling on foot for many days and nights, we now call the Denver Snow Shelter home ... at least for the time being. I can't explain how, in a time of such desperation, I was able to conveniently—brilliantly, if I say so—come up with the idea to come here. Luckily it was still intact. And I've been thankful for this space every moment of the last two days ... even if we've yet to figure out the many unexplained noises we continue to hear. We often wonder if it's the shelter or just the world itself trying to decide if it's truly finished with the horror it has unleashed.

I sat up and stretched, ready to continue working on our new normal—the new lives that we would build. The road to completing our goal was going to be rough. But with Cecilia—for Cecilia—I'd be able to accomplish anything. I was sure of it. I rolled myself out of bed and made my way over to the closet-sized bathroom.

I stared at my reflection and tried to figure out how a guy like me was still alive after this devastating earth alteration. My face looked scruffy since I hadn't shaved since the quake. My hair was getting too long, and the blond was fading more into a lighter brown, almost auburn. My arms were firm, and I had defined muscles in all the right places. My eyes, still a bright blue, never failed to be the biggest charmer for Cecilia. My girl.

I debated whether or not to hop in the shower or go see if she was awake.

Since we'd been here, I'd taken at least nine showers, taking advantage of the plentiful hot water. A very nice luxury considering the current state of affairs. Maybe it was too indulgent? I wasn't sure how long our luck would last.

It was so unbelievably hard to man-up and comfort Cecilia when I could barely stand the horrible conditions myself. All in all, I was just glad the initial struggle to survive was over. We were safe for the time being.

I decided against showering and instead went to see if Cecilia was awake. I walked out into the hallway and tiptoed up to her bedroom door. I knocked and waited a moment to see if she would answer. She didn't. I turned the doorknob and peeked inside. Her bed was perfectly made, and she was nowhere to be seen. I rolled my eyes. She'd always been the tidiest girl I'd ever known.

...For more, get your copy of The Inside, Book 2 today!